Little Red Riding Hood.

Into the Forest Again

Sincere thanks and gratitude are expressed to my family and friends, and to early and final readers of this manuscript—Judy Torres, Becca Barlow, Sara Olds, Melanie Skelton, Debbie Nance, C Zebleckes, and S Wilczak—your encouragement kept me moving forward.

First paperback edition, March 2011
Essemkay Company Productions
ISBN 9780615445977
LCCN 2011925211

This is a work of fiction, based on the author's imagination.

...Visit www.shaundawenger.blogspot.com ...

Little Red Riding Hood.

Into the Forest Again

By

Shaunda Kennedy Wenger

For Katherine, Margot, and Emma,

who love to dress up and dance.

May you always find your way

to Grandmother's house.

Contents

1 Dilly Dally

In an old, little house, near an old, little forest, a cake platter sat on a shoe box next to the door. Above him, a mirror hung on the wall.

Together, they waited and listened to the makings of morning—the pouring of milk, the clinking of spoons, the munching of toast with grape jelly—until at long last, a bright red coat was lifted from its hook in the hall.

It was lifted by Little Red, the girl of the house, who liked to wear little red coats.

Little Red liked to wear other things, too, like red bows in her hair, and red dresses trimmed in white, and white socks trimmed in red, and a little yellow flower tucked behind her ear. . . .

A yellow flower was always tucked behind her ear. Little Red stopped at the mirror to admire it.

"You look like a princess!" the mirror said.

"I'm glad of that," Little Red said, "because I'm on my way to a feast for one."

"A feast! Yes, a feast! And I shall be the center of it!"

Little Red turned to Platter. He held a tip-top, big blue cake. He grinned, as she bent over him and breathed in.

Yummies of strawberry, lemon, cherry, and plum, coconut, kiwi, and blue-buttery-fun filled up her nose, spread through her mouth, and tickled her all the way to the top of her head. She felt like she had just filled her tummy with a big slice.

But she hadn't.

No, Little Red hadn't tasted a speck of it, yet. *That* would happen at Grandmother's house.

"Well, don't dilly!" said the mirror.

"You mean, don't dally," said Little Red.

The mirror chuckled. "Both," he said.

"Ah, yes. We won't dilly, nor dally. Better yet, we won't dilly-dally. Isn't that right, my proud, little platter?"

"Quite right," he replied. "Not in these woods."

The mirror nodded. His mood changed, as Little Red tied her hood. "Oh, I do wish your mother could go."

"Mother went to market. But Grandmother will be waiting. I'll be fine."

"Well, don't talk to strangers."

Little Red tsked. "Don't talk to strangers, don't talk to strangers." She tossed her head. "Why worry about strangers? A *wolf* caused all the trouble last time."

"A strange wolf," said the mirror.

"A *big, bad* wolf," added Platter, "who liked to wear Grandmother's clothes. You shouldn't have talked to him."

Little Red huffed. "Yes, yes, we all know that. No need to bring it up again. I won't talk to strangers, unless I need to. Which I won't," she added, seeing the mirror's look of alarm. "After all, I *am* in a hurry. I'm on my way to a party!"

"And a good one at that," the mirror said, wiping away his worry with a wink. "And just between us, it's *you*—not that platter—who shall be the center of it."

Little Red laughed. She picked up the platter and walked outside.

Not one of them—the girl with her coat, the mirror with its shiny pane, nor the platter with its cake—saw the shadow that slipped over the window, as she went.

2 Heavy Darkness

Little Red marched down the path, singing, while her coat swished along.

"Hi ho! Hi ho! To Grandma's house I go! With a grand old cake and my little red coat! Hi ho! Hi ho, hi ho, hi ho!"

She sang this song over and over.

But it wasn't long before the happy singing was replaced by more careful singing; and then, the more careful singing by none at all.

Because as it often happens to girls walking alone, no matter how brave they try to be, singing can get filled up by an *icky, sick-feeling* when the forest begins to change.... When the trees along the path grow taller and THICKER; when the light from above grows darker and HEAVIER; and when the air all around grows sharper and COOLER.

Yes, that is what happened, as Little Red walked deeper into the woods.

And as all of these things happened, they wrapped *everything* up in a VERY BIG quiet.

A scary type of quiet.

The kind of quiet that makes every sound—the SNAP! of a twig, the FLAP! of a wing, the CAW! of a bird—all the more snappier, and all the more flappier, and all the more caw-CAW-CAWier.

Little Red tried to make herself small and unnoticeable.

Her steps became teensy.

Her eyes became squinty.

Her shoulders became hunchy.

But none of these things helped.

Little Red's fear grew.

In fact, her fear grew so much, Little Red thought it'd come pounding right out of her head.

Feeling Little Red's steps slow, Platter tried to stand taller to boost up his cake and remind Little Red of where they were going.

But Platter couldn't get taller than a pinch past an inch—which was exactly how tall he already was.

Little Red's steps slowed even more.

Platter tried to stretch forward, thinking he might pull her along.

"What's wrong?" he asked. "We agreed not to dally, remember?"

"Hush!" she replied. She looked over her shoulder. "I saw something."

"All the more reason to keep moving, then."

But Little Red stopped on the path.

What should she do? Go back home? Drop the cake and run?

Because no matter how small and unnoticeable Little Red could become, she knew there was nothing she could do about the yummies of strawberry, lemon, cherry, and plum, coconut, kiwi and blue-buttery-fun floating along and mixing with the shadows around her.

Yummies like that are very noticeable, even to the tiniest of creatures.

And so, while Little Red stood on the path, wondering if she should walk forward or run back, she and the cake got noticed.

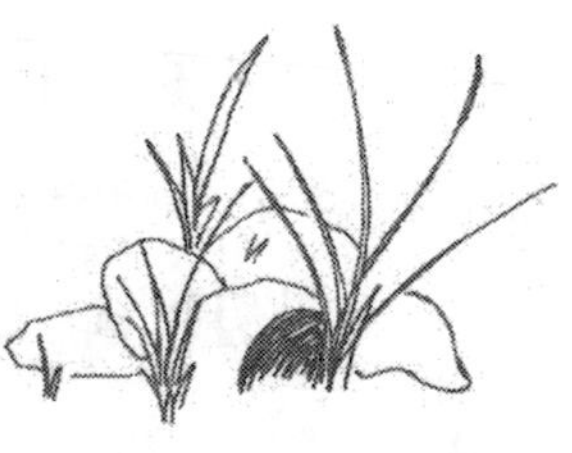

3 Shades of Gray

Bitty Gray poked his pink nose out from his hole in the rock wall and took a long sniff.

Then he took another.

And another.

But rather than sniff again—although he wanted to—Bitty Gray pushed himself out of his hole and ran on to the path.

Bitty Gray was a mouse. A tiny mouse with teeny, round ears and teeny, yellow claws.

In fact, not only was he teeny-tiny, he was downright puny. So puny, some might say he was the tiniest creature of the forest.

But despite his small size, Bitty Gray could make something big.

Squeaks.

And peeps—*and thank goodness.*

Because if it weren't for his clear cries of hello, Little Red would have squished him flat.

"Excus-zay!" Bitty Gray squeaked. "Excus-zay!"

Little Red peered around the side of her cake.

"Down here! Down here!" Bitty Gray cried.

Catching her eye with a wave of his blue cap, he pressed on. "Pray-tell, what is that yummy-yum-yum? Hmmmm? Five tip-top layers of blue-buttery-fun! All carried by one little girl? Surely, you have a crumb to share? Surely, one crumb?"

Seeing that it was a mouse who called her attention, Little Red sighed with relief.

Bitty Gray wrinkled his nose and sniffed, waiting for an answer.

Although Bitty Gray was teeny, he could still feel hungry. And at that moment, he was very hungry, indeed. Smelling the cake made him feel hungrier.

Platter snorted. He knew nothing of hunger. "A crumb?" he said. "Of course, there will be crumbs. But you are a mouse. What place do you have at a party for a princess? That is where this cake is going."

"Listen to you!" said Little Red. "How can you say that to this bitty gray thing, when *we* may not even get there?"

"Not get to the par—!?!"

Little Red put a hand over Platter's mouth.

"Excuse my friend," she said, bending down to Bitty Gray. "He is a plate of wood—thick in thought and flat in head."

"Nod ged do da par-day?!" Platter had squeezed his lips through her fingers.

"Yes, not make it to the party." Little Red moved her hand. "It seems like a long way to go just for tea."

"But I can't miss this party!" Platter said with a cry. "I'm the center-piece!"

"You can be the center-piece at home."

"But it's a party for a princess!"

"A foolish princess, you mean."

Bitty Gray cleared his throat. He held his cap to his chest. "Excus-zay, dear Princess, where are you wanting to go?"

Hearing the name, "Princess," Little Red let a smile curl on her lips. "We're going to Grandmother's house. It's on the other side of the forest."

Bitty Gray took in a breath, as if he hadn't taken one in a long time. Then he let it out with a low whistle. "The other side of the forest," he repeated. "I've heard of it. It's not too long a way. There's a party, you say?"

"Yes," Platter cried. "And we can't miss it! I won't miss it!"

Little Red scoffed. "What shall you do? Walk there on your own?"

Bitty Gray put his cap on his head. "Perhaps you'd like some company on your walk? Company in exchange for crumbs?"

Little Red thought for a moment. "Crumbs for company?"

Bitty Gray nodded. "Good company can be hard to find in a forest."

"Well, to be honest, the serving of crumbs is for Grandmother to decide. And I've never seen a mouse in her kitchen. But perhaps, that can change.... Are you of good manners and fine repute? That would rest in your favor."

Bitty Gray pulled at his whiskers to straighten them. He stretched up on the balls of his toes. He curled his tail and tapped his cap. "I have good manners, but what does 'fine repute' mean?"

"It means you are known to be nice."

"Oh, yes, I am," said Bitty Gray.

"Okay, then. We can try trading crumbs for company."

And so, at Little Red's nod, they set off, with Little Red making her steps quick and light, Bitty Gray sniffing those yummies of fun, and Platter tipping forward—just a wee little bit—as if he were leading the way.

Of all the shadows pressing around, one moved steadily along.

4 Bits of Brown

Big Bad peered from the trunk of a tree and watched Little Red with her cake.

She licked her licky-lick lips.

She rapped her tappy-tap claws.

She twitched her twitchy-twitch tail.

"Scrummmptious," she said with a growl. "Scrummmptious! Yummmptious! Yummy-yum-yummmmm!"

Big Bad sniffed again. "May need a touch of salt, though."

"A touch of what?" asked Snake. He was curled on a rock near the tree.

"Salt. But never mind." Big Bad shook her head. She hadn't known anyone would be listening. No one ever listened to her—not unless she was howling at the moon.

Howling. That's what other wolves called it. But not her. Big Bad liked to say she was singing.

Big Bad loved singing. *Awoooooooo*! she sang.

And people listened.

When she wasn't singing, Big Bad was more like a fly on a tree. A quiet, *sneaky* fly who never had much to say. That's because Big Bad liked *sneaking* around.

And wolves who sneak around try to be quiet.

Big Bad was good at being quiet.

She was also good at thinking.

(Thinking is what quiet, sneaky wolves do.)

Lately, Big Bad had done lots of thinking—about how to get Little Red with her cake.

Making her voice sing-song low, Big Bad leaned toward Snake and said, "I'm on my way, I'm on my way, I'm on my way to Grandmother's house."

"Is that so? Ssssssss." Snake flicked his tongue. "Lucky for you, the woods-man is on the other side of the forest. Ssssssss."

Big Bad snarled. "Why do you say that?"

"I've heard of you. Ssssssss. Or, someone like you. Ssssssss. Who met the woods-man and his axe. Ssssssss."

Big Bad paced a small circle in the dirt. "That's why I stay on this side of the forest. I keep clear of that axe."

"Ssssssss." Snake curled like a rope.

Big Bad stooped toward him again. "Would you like, would you like, would you like to go with me? Would you like to go with me to Grandmother's house?"

"Sssssssss, no."

"Are you sure?"

"Sssssssss, yes. You're blocking my sun."

Giving a sigh, Big Bad left Snake in his small patch of sun.

Soon enough, Big Bad was sneaking along again. And soon after that, Big Bad started to hum. It was a quiet little hum that went with her sneaky, little thoughts.

One—grrrrr. I must dress for the party. I must dress. I must dress. I must dress.

Two—grrrrr. I must hide in the shade. I must hide. I must hide. I must hide.

Three—grrrrr. I must comb all my fur. I must comb. I must comb. I must comb.

Four—grrrrr. I must listen for feet, the patter of feet, the patter-pat-patter of feet. When I hear the patter of feet, it will be time for Big Bad to eat!

Yummm-yummmmm!

5 Hops of Blue

Bright Blue sat in a fir tree high above a river bend, watching two groups of travelers make their way through the forest. One walked on the path. The other darted from tree to tree, until it ran on ahead.

Usually, Bright Blue didn't pay much attention to what passed below. Travelers walked on the path every day, and the forest was full of creatures that liked to stay out of sight. But that morning, the group on the path held his attention.

Bright Blue couldn't turn his head from the jewels that shimmered on the cake.

"I could use them," he said with a short, little hop. "I could use them to find a mate."

Bright Blue had built a nest. He hadn't had any luck finding another bird to share it with.

"Tucking a few shims in my nest would help."

He swooped above Little Red's head. "Twitter be!" he said. "Twitter you be going with those shimmy-shim-shims?"

Little Red peered up from the side of her cake. She was relieved to see it was a bird calling her attention.

Platter, who was upset at stopping, scowled again. "Shims, you say? *Shims*? What shims?" He tipped himself in Little Red's hands and squinted at the top of the

cake. "These *jewels*, you mean?" He tsked at the bird. "They're going to a party for a princess!"

Little Red couldn't help but smile. Her mood had lightened at the sight of the pretty bird.

Bright Blue landed in a nearby tree. He didn't want to believe what this meant—that there'd be no giving of shims!

"What would a jittery bird like you do with *jewels*?" Platter asked.

Bright Blue fluffed his wings. "I need them for my nest."

"Nest? Hmmph! Nest, indeed!" Platter gave Bright Blue a hard look. "I dare say, you should be on your way. Birds might be plucked for our party today."

"Oh, Platter, tie your tongue." Little Red shook her head. "First of all, these aren't jewels on the cake; they're candy. Secondly, this bird is no more jittery than me or the mouse. And thirdly, no one I know has ever plucked feathers."

Bitty Gray gave Bright Blue a nod. "You'll have to excuse him," he said, tipping his chin twice at the platter. "He is a plate of wood—flat in thought and thick in head."

"*Thick in thought* and *flat in head*, you mean," said Little Red.

"Yes, that's it," said Bitty Gray with a grin.

Platter tried to speak, but Little Red held a hand to his mouth.

"What we mean to say," she continued, "is that the serving of shims is for someone else to decide—*my grandmother*. She is hosting the party. However, she is quite kind, and she doesn't pluck feathers. Not for her hat, nor for her bed."

Bright Blue whistled. "I know of your grandmother!" He flew to another low branch. "I've collected seed from her feeders and bugs from her garden."

"You're a thief, then?"

"Oh, Platter." Little Red closed his mouth again.

"No, not a thief—a good helper!" said Bright Blue. "I eat pests!"

The platter cringed.

"Sounds like a good guest to me," said Bitty Gray.

"Yes, I agree," Little Red whispered back. "But I suppose, to be fair, I'll have to ask him what I asked you."

She turned to Bright Blue. "Are you of good manners and fine repute, little bird? It would rest in your favor."

"I'm never anything less," he replied. "And since I don't like taking without giving in return, shall we make a trade? A pair of bright eyes for some shimmy-shim-shims?"

"Eyes! We don't want your eyes!" Platter cried.

"That is a bit drastic," said Little Red.

"Don't you need them?" asked Bitty Gray.

Bright Blue twittered. "No, no. I meant I could be your eyes in the sky! A guide along the way. I can see a long way above the trees."

"Hmmmm. Eyes for shims...." Little Red twirled with the cake. "I can't make any promises, but if you'd like to take your chances—."

Little Red stopped, hearing the loud snap of a twig.

And then another.

The snaps came from the wooded bog nearby.

"Wh-what was that?" Platter asked.

Little Red pulled him close to her chest, taking care not to crush the blue cake.

Bitty Gray rubbed his fur to keep it from standing on end. But it was no use. As the noises got closer, his fur got stiffer, until it felt like he was covered in spikes.

Little Red stepped back to the edge of the path. She didn't know what to fear more—the rustling from the bushes, or the cold, wet darkness that pressed closer and closer around her.

6 Nips of Tan, Tips of White

Jolly Round had smelled cake. Cake was not something he smelled very often in the forest.

His friend Flat O'Foot did not smell cake—or, at least, not very much of it.

That is because Flat O'Foot was a duck, and he didn't have a nose. He had a beak—which is too bad. He would have loved smelling the strawberry, lemon, cherry, and plum, coconut, kiwi and blue-buttery fun, almost as much as Jolly Round did.

But it didn't matter.

Flat O'Foot loved his porcupine friend. He copied Jolly Round in everything he did.

So, when Jolly Round breathed in a second time and smiled, Flat O'Foot did the same.

And when Jolly Round tipped his head, listening to talk of cake *and a party*, Flat O'Foot held his head at attention.

Flat O'Foot loved parties. Almost as much as Jolly Round loved cake.

Butterflies began to bop in his belly.

Tingles began to tickle his toes.

Wiggles began to whip through his wings.

Flat O'Foot wiggled so much, he felt he'd start dancing on air.

But he didn't.

He kept his feet flat on the ground.

This was the thickest and darkest part of the forest, and Flat O'Foot wasn't good at flying in it.

Not wanting to miss out on cake, nor a party, he did what he did second-best. He ran.

Yes, that's right. Flat O'Foot led the way—bashing through brambles and crashing through reeds. Within moments, both he and Jolly Round burst from the bog and tumbled onto the path.

Little Red nearly fainted with relief. After all, it was only a fat porcupine and a chubby, white duck that had made all that noise.

Jolly Round stood as quick as he could. He smoothed his tan quills and pinched up his cheeks in a grin. "I am a well-mannered fellow!" he cried.

"And I am of no bad repute!" Flat O'Foot added. "Although, I'm not sure I

know what that means! But that cake that you tote, with its nutty-blue-fun—!"

"And its berry-yum-yum!" said Jolly Round. "All carried by one little girl? Surely, you can spare a nip?"

"A nip?" asked Little Red, still catching her breath.

"A nibble, or two," said Flat O'Foot, pressing his beak into a smile.

"Or four," said Jolly Round, giving Flatty a nudge.

"Shhh! That's rude!"

Flat O'Foot gave Little Red a bow. "What we mean is, for ourselves, surely there are enough nips for two?"

The duck and the porcupine bowed as low as they could; because for a flat-footed duck that eats weeds and a jolly-round porcupine that eats bark, the thought of a tiny taste of a sugary cake seemed more than they could hope for.

Little Red studied them. "Surely, you know what I'll say? You seem to know a lot already."

"Maybe... but a duck of fine repute would not dare assume."

"Nor, would a well-mannered fellow... errr... my Sweet Princess, and—uh, Dear Thick One, who is too flat-of-head."

Bright Blue and Bitty Gray tried not to chuckle.

Flat O'Foot lifted his webby toe at Platter. "And look at this! I am flat-of-foot! We share something in common!"

Little Red laughed. "You did overhear. Very well. You may come along. I believe we're nearly there, aren't we?" She looked up at Bright Blue, who flew to the treetops.

"Yes!" he cried. "There's a small house in the distance! It looks lovely. Smoke is whispering from the chimney. Pink ribbons are dangling from the eaves. Flowers are blooming in the windows. And your grandmother is dancing in the yard!"

"Really?"

"Yes, yes, and what a fine coat she is wearing!"

Little Red's excitement grew. "Is it like mine?"

"Uh... not quite." Bright Blue glanced toward the house. "Funny... it's rather hot for that kind of coat today."

"What's that? I didn't hear you!"

"I said it's too hot for a coat!"

"It is? I didn't think so."

"She's also wearing a pretty pink skirt, and a pretty pink hat, and a pretty pink...." Bright Blue stopped on a branch.

Little Red raised her eyebrows. "A pretty pink what?"

"Forgive me," Bright Blue called down, "but I was going to say that your grandmother has a pretty pink tongue!"

"Tongue!" said Platter. "Of course, she's got a tongue!"

"Yes, but I've never seen it so big! She— she must be tired from dancing! It's hanging down out of her mouth!"

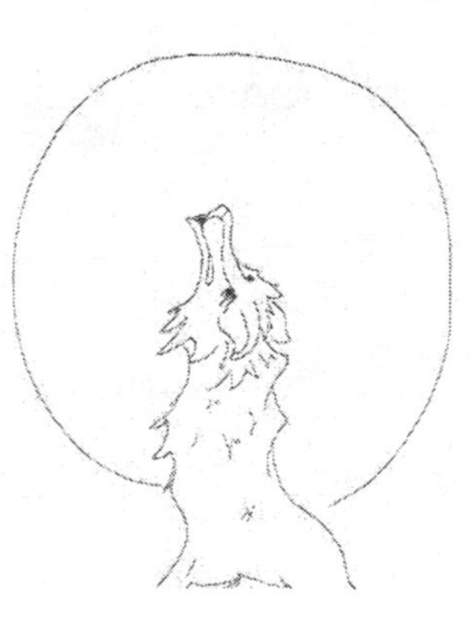

7 Taps in Time

Taking a break, Big Bad lay down and scratched her claws in the dirt.

Then she scratched again.

And again.

Big Bad was tired of waiting for Grandmother to show up at the door. She was tired of waiting for Little Red to come with her cake. Worse, her stomach kept grumbling, begging for the feast to begin.

Big Bad pressed her ear to the dirt.

After a moment, her claws began to tap. *Tap-tap-tapper-tap-tap. Tap-tap-tapper-tap-tap.*

Big Bad heard the *pat-pat-patter-pat-pat* of feet.

"Awoooooooo!" she sang softly.

And then she sang again.

And again.

Until she decided she had better keep quiet.

Unfortunately, it was too late.

Someone in the forest had heard.

8 Thoughts of Red

Hearing the howl—odd and light as it was—Grandmother looked up from the logs she was cutting. She wiped her forehead with the back of her hand. She'd heard howls before, but never at the peak of day. And never this close to the house.

Rubbing her old, crooked hands on her blue checkered dress, Grandmother's thoughts turned to Little Red. She'd be coming from the forest. It worried her that a wolf might be near.

Hearing the howl a second time, Grandmother kicked the dirt from her boots and reached for her axe. It'd been a gift from a woods-man. He'd made sure she knew how to use it.

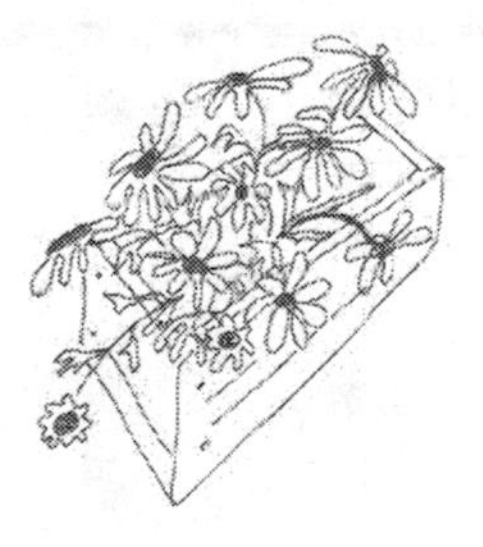

9 Spins in Pink

Taking a deep breath, Little Red stepped from the forest. The house looked just like Bright Blue had described. Smoke whispered from the chimney. Ribbons dangled from the eaves. Flowers bloomed at the windows. And her grandmother danced in the yard.

As Little Red watched, a smile spread on her face. But as she watched longer, Little

Red felt her smile slip away like hot butter from a knife. Fear twisted inside her.

That was not *Grandmother* dancing in the yard!

That was a wolf! A *strange* wolf! Who liked to wear little-girl-clothes!

Yes, that is what Little Red thought, given the small size of the tutu.

But actually, Little Red was wrong.

The clothes had never belonged to a girl. They belonged to the wolf. In fact, she'd made them that morning.

While Little Red liked to wear red, Big Bad had always wanted to wear pink, especially to a party. This one, she was hoping, would be her first, even if her skirt was too tight.

Seeing Little Red at the edge of the forest, Big Bad began galloping toward her.

Platter—nervous, as he was—tried to make a joke. "I suppose we'll find Grandmother in a closet?"

"Hush!" Little Red replied. Her voice was barely louder than a whisper. "Nobody move."

They all did the best they could.

Little Red and Bitty Gray shivered.

Bright Blue and Jolly Round quivered.

But Flat O'Foot? He fell flat on his rear.

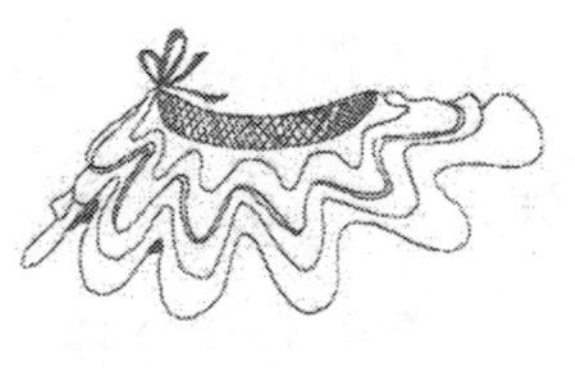

10 Nerves on Edge

Big Bad skidded to a stop before them and made a tight turn on her toes. Spinning in her skirt, she sang, "Oh, do say, grrrrr-grrrrr, oh, do say, grrrrr-grrrrr, oh, do say I can come to your party, grrrrr-grrrrr!"

No one replied. Not even Platter.

"I... uh...." Little Red was so frightened, she could hardly speak. Focusing on Big

Bad's pink crown, she said, "You want to come to my party?"

"Yes, grrrrr. For one little bite?"

"A bite?" Little Red pressed closer to the others around her.

Big Bad nodded and spun such a tight circle, her crown fell off her head.

Little Red shuffled her feet and moved a teensy step back, trying not to trip over Jolly Round. "Oh, no. I don't think... I'm not sure."

Platter coughed once, spit twice.

Not knowing what else to do, Little Red held him up with a sigh.

"My dear, Furball," Platter began. "You are a wolf. Wolves are known for bad manners. Wolves are known for their big, bad repute. Surely, you don't think you can come to our party! This party is for a princess, and we're late!"

Big Bad began to cry. "But I love cake! And I have tried so hard to be good, grrrrr. I

have tried so hard to change my reputation, grrrrr-grrrrr. I'm not like other wolves. All I've ever wanted is a good slice of cake, along with an invitation to a party!"

Tears streamed from her eyes and dripped on the ground. "Strawberry, lemon, cherry, and plum," Big Bad said sadly. She picked up her crown and put it on Little Red's head. "Coconut, kiwi, and blue-buttery-fun.... To think I thought I could come."

Jolly Round coughed. "She does have the dress for it."

Platter jeered. "A strange dress! Do I need to remind you of whom this is?"

"And she did make the crown for it," Flat O'Foot said, tugging on Little Red's coat.

Platter spat. "No matter!"

"She has the teeth for it, too," twittered Bright Blue in Little Red's ear.

Big Bad bared her teeth. "Yes, they're all fake. Every last one. I love sweets! I can't live without them!"

"Sounds like a regular sweet-tooth to me," squeaked Bitty Gray, his stomach growling.

"Wait, wait, wait!" said Platter. "Doesn't anyone ever listen to me! We can't have HER at the party! She's a wolf! I'm the center—."

"Yes, yes, we know. You're the center-piece," said Little Red. "And a very fine center-piece you'll be. But just as we *oooh* and *ahhh* for the center-piece, the center-piece must *oooh* and *ahhh* at the guests. Now look at everything this wolf has done for the party. She's wearing a pretty tutu. She's made a pretty crown. She's even danced a pretty dance."

Big Bad tried to shuffle her feet, but she was too sad.

Little Red gave Big Bad a hanky. She put the pink crown back on Big Bad's head.

"I might as well tell you," she said with a sigh. "The serving of cake is up to Grandmother. She's never known a wolf with good manners, but perhaps, if you can be nice, the rest will fall into favor."

The group nodded around her, feeling a bit odd. After all, Big Bad was a wolf.

But even wolves can change, if they want to.

And so can platters.

Platter tipped his head in agreement. He even tried a small smile. "What are we waiting for? Let's see this wolf dance for—"

"—me."

The group turned.

Grandmother stood on the path with her axe.

11 Checks in Blue

Grandmother dug one heel in the dirt, squishing tiny circles with it. Her blue checkered dress billowed out at the knees—looking, she knew, like laundry on the line.

But that was the least of her worries. Her biggest worry was Little Red, who was standing next to a wolf and other strange creatures.

Grandmother twisted the axe in her hands. "I only sent one invitation! How did so many happen to come?"

Little Red tried a nervous smile. "They're hungry, you see... and it was such a long walk through the forest, along the way I found company."

Grandmother laughed. "My dear child, you have a wolf with you."

"Yes, but look at her. We... we were just talking about that." Little Red paused.

"Talking about what?"

"The wolf... and this cake... and whether we would share?"

Grandmother's eyes went wide.

"The others are hungry, too. This is Bitty Gray." Little Red scooped him up. "And he and I made a deal to trade crumbs for company."

Bitty Gray tipped his cap. "Just a crumb will do. It's a pleasure to meet you."

Grandmother nodded.

"And then we met Bright Blue, who needs shims for his nest."

"I was their guide," he said, fluttering on the path. "But we've met before. I eat the bad bugs in your garden."

Grandmother gave him a smile.

Flat O'Foot cleared his throat. "And then Little Red met *us*. We begged for a nip—"

"—and a nibble," finished Jolly Round, placing his arm on his friend. "In return, we'd be happy to trim a hedge, or dig up a bramble. We have a fine set of teeth and beak between us."

Grandmother shook her head in amusement.

Her cheeriness didn't last long. Big Bad stood shaking before her, eyeing the length of her axe.

"And now, here's this wolf, wanting no more than a bite?" Grandmother crossed her arms. "I must say, I wasn't expecting a creature like you."

"I know." Big Bad fiddled with the pleats of her tutu. "I also know you weren't expecting anyone else, except Little Red, which is why I ran ahead and got everything ready."

Grandmother looked back at the house in surprise. The smoke billowing from the chimney wasn't from her fire. The flowers blooming at the windows weren't her daisies. The pink ribbons dangling from the eaves weren't her ribbons, at all.

No, if Grandmother had thought to hang ribbons, she would have hung blue. But still, they did look nice.

"You did that?" Grandmother said, sweeping her arm at the house.

Big Bad nodded. "And the table is set inside. The drinks are made. And a riser is waiting for the center-piece." Big Bad shot Platter a small smile.

"You made a platform for me?" he asked.

"All the better to seat you at," Big Bad replied.

"Well," said Grandmother. "Blow me over with wishes. This is a far cry from any big, bad wolf I know. What do you think, Little Red?"

Little Red twirled in her little red cape. "First, I think her name doesn't suit her. From now on, I shall call her Big Good.

"Second, I think she has shown nothing but fine manners and good repute. And that's all anyone needs to come to a party.

"And third, I think I'd like to see Big Good dance. She seems gifted in that way."

With that, the odd group set off, with Little Red leading the way and Big Good leading their song.

"Hi ho! To Grandma's house we go! With friends and a cake and a coat and a skirt! Hi ho! Hi ho, hi ho, hi ho!"

As it turned out, there was more than a crumb, and a shim, and a nip, and nibble, and a bite, and a slice of that tasty cake for everyone.

About the Author

I grew up running through the woods of New Hampshire, where I fell in love with nature, art, and all its forms. The story of "Little Red Riding Hood" was one of my favorites. I loved Little Red for her bravery and good intentions in wanting to walk through the forest to visit her grandmother. This new story came to me one sunny day in February 2007. I loved each of the characters as they met Little Red, but Big Bad surprised me the most.

Learn more at
www.shaundawenger.blogspot.com

CPSIA information can be obtained at www.ICGtesting.com
Printed in the USA
LVOW041725110112

263410LV00001B/121/P

9 780615 445977